BIRDSONG

Story and Pictures by Gail E. Haley

Crown Publishers, Inc. New York

Published by Crown Publishers, Inc., One Park Avenue,
New York, New York 10016, and simultaneously in Canada
by General Publishing Company Limited. Manufactured in
Italy 10 9 8 7 6 5 4 3 2 1

Library of Congress Cataloging in Publication Data. Haley,
Gail E. Birdsong. Summary: "Befriended" by an old woman,
a grubby urchin soon discovers her evil intent, and with the
help of bird friends delivers a well-deserved comeuppance.
[1. Birds—Fiction] I. Title. PZ7.H1383Bi 1984 [E] 83-14372
ISBN 0-517-55051-2

*This story happened long ago
and far away, but you can still
hear its echoes in the dawn chorus
of the birds. They love to tell
how greedy Jorinella outwitted herself.*

Jorinella took her wicker stall to the marketplace and arranged the cages of birds that she had caught with her limed strings and bamboo traps. By mid-morning all the birds were sold.

Her customers grumbled, "You never bring as many birds as you used to."

"Why, there are hardly enough wrens here for a pie."

"What's the trouble, Jorinella, are you losing your touch or just getting old?" they taunted her.

Jorinella tried to ignore the villagers' words as she packed her empty cages into her cart and then headed toward the baker's stall. She had barely enough money for two of her favorite cakes.

As she turned to walk toward the village green, she noticed a ragged young girl sitting on a bench, playing her pipes.

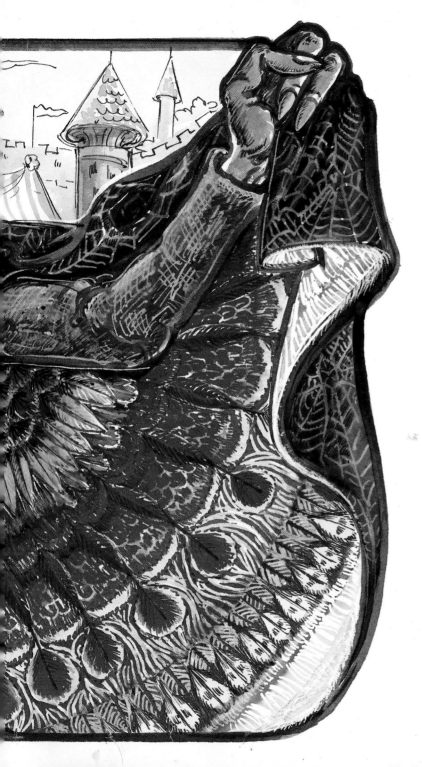

The girl was playing an old ballad, and her begging bowl lay empty beside her. She was so lost in her music she did not notice that the trees around her and the pavement at her feet were filled with wild birds that had come to join in with her playing.

Jorinella's eyes lit up. A plan was forming in her mind as she handed the girl one of the cakes. "Who are you, my pet," she crooned, "and why are you here all alone?"

"I am an orphan without a true name or home," the girl answered timidly. "I am always alone."

"Ah. Well, I shall call you Birdsong," Jorinella said. "I too live alone and I am growing old. Come with me, help me with my chores, and you can have all that I own—even my cloak."

Jorinella spread her cloak wide; it was lined with the feathers of birds and glowed with every color of the rainbow.

Something about the old woman frightened Birdsong, but the beauty of the cloak and the fragrance of the cake were more than the hungry girl could resist.

"Yes, Grandmother, I will come with you," she said.

Birdsong climbed into Jorinella's cart and rode with her deep into the forest. As soon as they reached the old woman's hut, Jorinella bathed Birdsong in a steaming tub, cut the tangles from her hair, and braided it up out of her eyes. Then she opened an old trunk and took out a pretty but faded dress, just the right size for Birdsong. The girl put on the dress and looked at herself in a polished glass that Jorinella held for her. No sign of the street urchin remained except for her pipes.

Amazed at what she saw, Birdsong whispered, "No one has ever done anything nice for me before; how can I ever repay you?"

"I told you I'm not as spry as I once was," Jorinella answered. "You can help me clean the house, gather wood, and keep the stew bubbling while I'm away. Here, have a bit of supper now, and then try to go to sleep." With that Jorinella herself went to bed.

But Birdsong stayed awake for a long time, staring into the fire. She could not imagine what further wonders the next day would bring.

In the morning Jorinella took Birdsong out into the forest. She pulled a package from a hidden pocket of her cloak and handed it to the girl. Inside was the most beautiful feather Birdsong had ever seen.

"This is a magic feather," Jorinella told her. "When you wear it, it will open your ears and your heart. You will be able to understand the language of the birds and play their songs on your pipes."

Birdsong accepted the feather with trembling hands. Looking up in amazement, she realized that suddenly she truly could understand the birds.

She heard nesting songs of parents
with a clutch of smooth warm eggs.
She heard peeping songs of hatching
and lullabies for naked nestlings
snuggled beneath downy breasts.
There were breakfast songs for babies,
open-mouthed and always hungry;
fledgling rhymes for bright-eyed birdlings
coaxed to sit on swaying branches.
Every lilting song of newness
entered Birdsong's willing heart.

Birds have songs for every feeling;
Birdsong learned to play them all.
She learned piping songs for soaring,
roaming melodies for flying,
crescendos for diving down
with flashing eyes and folded wings,
songs for stretching, hunting, preening.
She played the joyous new-day chorus
sung to welcome every dawn
and the crooning sleepy songs
that welcome moon and stars.
As if by magic, she seemed to share
the lives of all birdkind.

When the wild birds heard her piping, every feathered flying creature came to find Birdsong and to listen. Birdsong was happy. She had food, a warm bed, and the birds of the forest for her friends. And her skill on the pipes grew with each passing day.

But one event puzzled Birdsong as she went about her cleaning and tidying in the following weeks. She found an old set of pipes hidden away in the corner of a cupboard. They were very much like her own, except that they were cracked and dirty with misuse. She took them to Jorinella and asked, "Whose pipes are these?"

Jorinella took the pipes, fingering the faded scrap of ribbon that still clung to them. "They belong to someone who will never play them again," she said. "They are useless." But she put them on a shelf where she could see them from time to time.

Early one morning, Jorinella took Birdsong to a forest clearing, where she had built a little wicker hut covered with leaves.

She opened a door in the side of the hut. "I want you to go inside and play the songs you have learned," Jorinella told Birdsong. "I will be gathering herbs and berries in the forest, and the sound of your pipes will keep me from straying too far." Birdsong went inside the hut, and Jorinella locked the door behind her.

Birdsong sat inside the wicker hut and began to play. She poured out her feelings for the birds. She played the songs her feathered friends had taught her about their lives, flights, and joys. She played about her own joy, too, about the happiness her new life had given her. The birds heard the love and trust in her heart; flocks of them came flying.

They came from forests and deserts, mountains and seashores. Every kind of bird made its way to Birdsong's bower. And all the while that Birdsong played, Jorinella was busy with nets and snares, limed strings and bamboo traps.

It was dusk when Jorinella finally opened the door. Birdsong tumbled out, exhausted from her playing. As her eyes adjusted themselves to the waning light, she was horrified by what she saw. All around the wicker hut there were cages, piled on top of other cages, as far as she could see. They were filled with the birds who had come to hear her piping.

Jorinella danced around, clapping her hands. "I never had so many birds at one time," she chortled. Birdsong turned away and peered into one of the cages. She did not want Jorinella to see how she really felt about the trapped birds.

"I need you to stay here," Jorinella told Birdsong, "and guard the birds against robbers and wild animals. I'll be back first thing in the morning to collect the birds in my wagon."

As Jorinella walked away, dreaming about the money she would make, she did not notice that a feather had fallen from her cloak. It was twisted, ugly, and dirty. Birdsong picked it up.

"Perhaps this too is a magic feather," she thought. "I wonder if there is anything it can do to help me now?"

A dark, sad secret flowed from the feather into Birdsong's thoughts. She saw—far back in time—a girl in a faded dress who played birds onto her fingers with the sweetness of her music. But then she saw how that girl had been overcome by greed and had sold the birds who were her friends. The name of that other girl was *Jorinella!*

Now the birds sang a song Birdsong had never heard before.

> They sang of hungry nestlings—alone,
> afraid—whimpering in the night;
> Love birds cried to mates left behind;
> Plump birds sobbed their fear of being eaten;
> Songbirds wailed to think of
> being locked forever in cages—to sing
> sad songs of their lost freedom.
> The nightingale wove all their songs
> into one melody of bird sorrow.

Birdsong opened some of the cages and called to the trapped birds to come out, but they tucked their heads under their wings, reminding her that birds cannot see to fly at night. The girl sat huddled among the cages, dreading Jorinella's return.

But at the first light of dawn Birdsong opened the door of a cage filled with blackbirds. They leapt into the air with joyous cries. From cage to cage she rushed, racing against Jorinella's return, to free all the captive birds. Soon the bushes, trees, and sky were filled with the freed birds, singing together the most magnificent dawn chorus the world has ever heard.

Just as the last bird was freed, Jorinella arrived at the clearing. She leapt from the wagon, a whip in her hand.

"You stupid, silly girl, how could you do this to me? We both could have been rich! You have betrayed me!"

"No, Jorinella. *You* have deceived *me* and all the innocent birds. I did not know you meant to profit from my music. During the night the birds told me how sweetly you used to play your pipes, until you became greedy and lured birds into your traps. Your heart grew hard; that is why you can no longer play the pipes I found."

Jorinella, her face dark with rage, raised her whip and flew at Birdsong.

"No one will ever hear your story; you will not return to tell it!"

But before she could do Birdsong any harm, the retreating birds saw what was happening. They flew at Jorinella, pecking, nipping, battering, and biting, until they drove her to the edge of the forest.

Some of the strongest birds, eagles, swans, and geese, caught up one of Jorinella's bird nets and lifted Birdsong into the sky. Up they flew, higher and higher until they were above the tallest trees. They could see the birdcatcher far below, shaking her fist and shouting for them to come back.

But the birds flew on, over forests, rivers, villages, and mountains, freeing Birdsong forever.

The birds flew until they came to a kingdom whose name is still a secret. Looking down, Birdsong could see that a celebration was going on. Flags were flying; people were dancing, singing, and playing instruments.

Down went the birds, into the middle of the festivities. People stared in amazement at the sight of the young girl descending from the sky. The birds flew around and around her, placing feathers in her hair and over her clothing until she was dressed in shining feathers from head to toe.

A group of musicians stopped their playing and came forward. They did not speak Birdsong's language, but when she played on her pipes, they gathered round to listen.

Birdsong taught them the songs she had learned from the birds. Together they built a beautiful garden where all the birds might come to sing and be heard.

This is not the end of the story. The kingdom still exists, hidden far away from prying eyes and unfriendly hearts. Only the birds know where it is. But if you listen carefully to their singing, perhaps they will show you where to find it.